WHO IS COMING TO OUR HOUSE?

By Joseph Slate
Pictures by Ashley Wolff

G. P. Putnam's Sons · New York

G. P. Putnam's Sons, a division of
The Putnam & Grosset Book Group, 200 Madison Avenue, New York, NY 10016. Sandcastle Books
and the Sandcastle logo are trademarks belonging to The Putnam & Grosset Book Group.
First Sandcastle Books edition published in 1991. Published simultaneously in Canada.
Printed in Singapore. Book design by Charlotte Staub.

Library of Congress Cataloging-in-Publication Data
Slate, Joseph. Who is coming to our house?
SUMMARY: The animals in the stable prepare for the arrival of baby Jesus.
1. Jesus Christ—Nativity—Juvenile fiction. [1. Animals—Fiction.
2. Jesus Christ—Nativity—Fiction.   3. Christmas—Fiction.   4. Stories in rhyme]
I. Wolff, Ashley, ill.   II. Title.   PZ8.3 .S629Wh   1988 [E] 87-7319
ISBN 0-399-21537-9 (hardcover)
7 9 10 8 6
ISBN 0-399-21790-8 (Sandcastle)
3 5 7 9 10 8 6 4

To Lisa, Marilyn, and Toni
J.S.

For my own little boy
A.W.

"Who is coming to our house?"
"Someone, someone," says Mouse.

"Make room," says Pig.

"I will butt aside the rig."

"We must clean," says Lamb.

"Dust the beams," says Ram.

"Someone,
someone,"
says Mouse.

"Sweep the earth," says Chick.

"Stack the hay," says Goose, "and quick!"

"Spin new webs," says Spider.

"I will line the crib with eider."

"Who is coming
to our house?"
"Someone, someone,"
says Mouse.

"Someone's coming from afar."

"I will nose the door ajar."

"But it is dark," says Cat.

"They will never come," says Rat.

"Yes, they'll come," says Mouse.
"Someone's coming to this house."

"I will lay an egg," says Hen.

"I will spread my tail for them."

"Who is coming to our house?"
"Mary and Joseph," whispers Mouse.

"Welcome, welcome to our house!"